For Andrea & Claudia
— I.F.

For Mum & Dad, who helped
— J.T.

LITTLE TIGER PRESS
An imprint of Magi Publications,
22 Manchester Street, London W1M 5PG

First published in 1999

The Very Lazy Ladybird

by Isobel Finn & Jack Tickle

LITTLE TIGER PRESS
London

This is the story of
a very lazy ladybird.

She liked to sleep all day . . .

and all night.

And because she slept
all day and all night,
this lazy ladybird didn't
know how to fly.

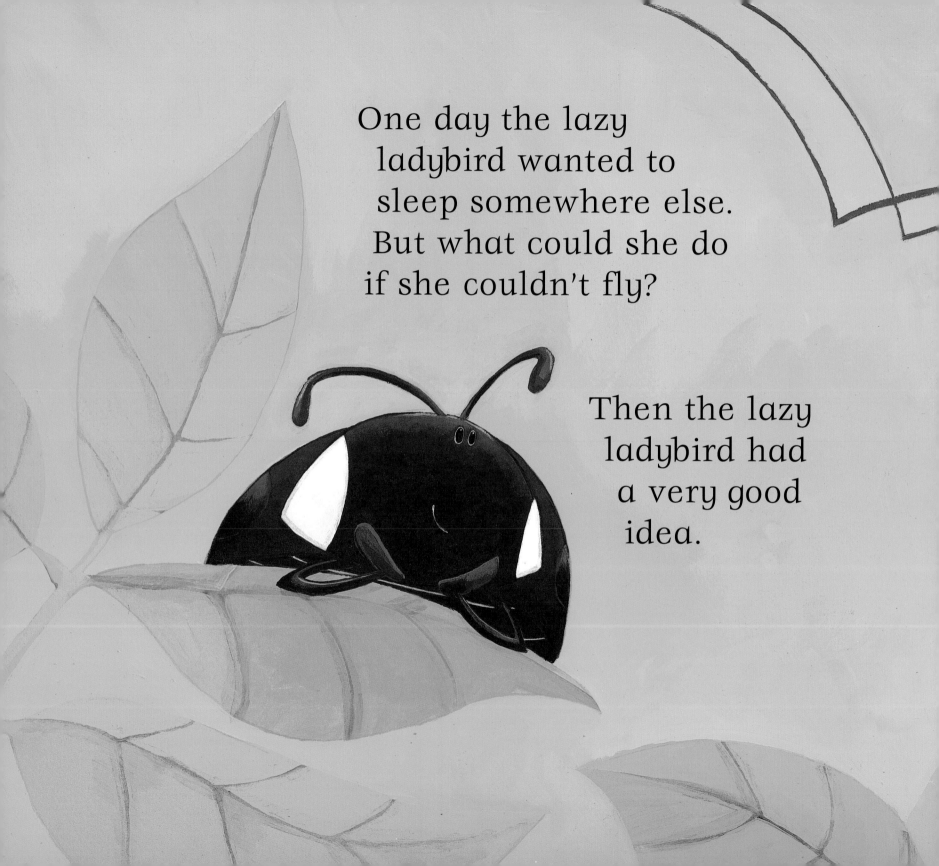

One day the lazy
ladybird wanted to
sleep somewhere else.
But what could she do
if she couldn't fly?

Then the lazy
ladybird had
a very good
idea.

When a kangaroo bounded by . . .

"I can't sleep in here,"
cried the lazy ladybird.
"It's far too bumpy."

so when a tiger padded by . . .

she hopped on to his back.

But the tiger liked to

ROAR!

"I can't sleep here,"
said the lazy ladybird.
"It's far too noisy."

So when a crocodile swam by . . .

she hopped on to his tail.

But the crocodile liked to

SWISH

his tail in the water.

"I can't sleep here,"
said the lazy ladybird.
"I'll fall into the river!"

So when a monkey swung by . . .

she hopped on to her head.

But the monkey liked to
SWING
from branch to branch.

"I can't sleep here,"
said the lazy ladybird.
"I'm feeling dizzy."

So when a bear ambled by . . .

she hopped on to his ear.

But the bear
liked to

SCRATCH!

"I can't sleep here,"
said the lazy ladybird.
"He'll never sit still."

So when a tortoise plodded by . . .

she hopped on to her shell.

But the tortoise liked to
S N O O Z E
in the sun.
"I can't sleep here,"
said the lazy ladybird.
"It's far too hot."

So when an elephant trundled by . . .

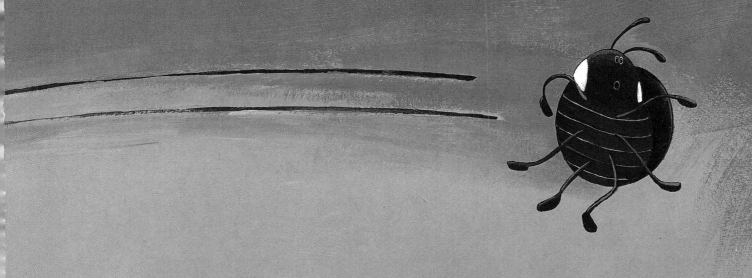

HOo

and poor old lazy ladybird . . .

But at that very moment . . .

the elephant

sneezed!

AAAC

had to fly at last!

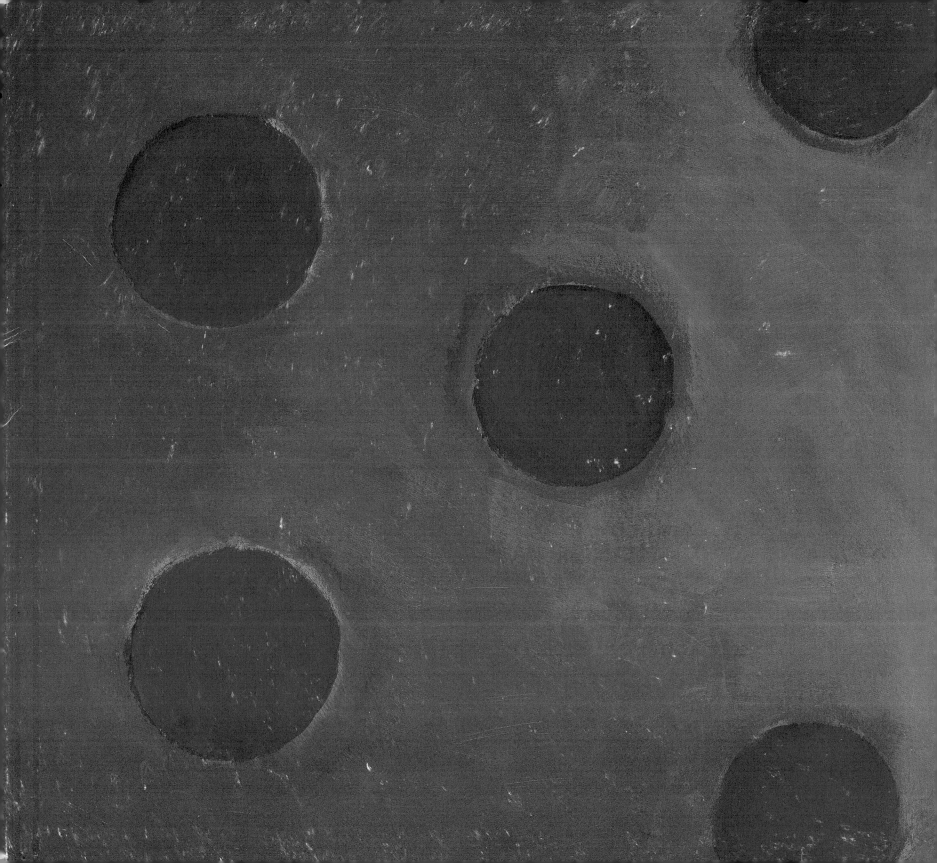